W9-CQZ-401

Copyright © 1990 by Modern Publishing, a division of
Unisystems, Inc.
Just for Me™ is a trademark of Modern
Publishing, a division of Unisystems, Inc.
® Honey Bear Books is a trademark owned by Honey Bear
Productions, Inc., and is registered in the U.S. Patent and
Trademark Office. All Rights Reserved.
No part of this book may be reproduced or copied without
written permission from the publisher.
Printed in Italy

JUST·FOR·ME ™

PROUD · PEACOCK

Written by Rosalyn Rosenbluth
Illustrated by Jo-Ellen Bosson

Modern Publishing
A Division of Unisystems, Inc.
New York, New York 10022

Proud Peacock is looking at himself in the water. "Do you think the blue in my third feather on the left is fading a little?" he asks Hungry Bear.

"Who cares?" says Hungry Bear.

Proud Peacock frowns. "You have good judgment," he says to Slow Turtle. "Do you think the blue in my third feather on the left is fading?"

Slow Turtle sighs. "It's my good judgment that you think entirely too much about your feathers," he replies.

Proud Peacock is angry. He tiptoes over to Gentle Lamb. "You're the only one here who appreciates a thing of beauty," he whispers in Gentle Lamb's ear. "Do you think the blue in my third feather on the left is fading—just a little?"

Gentle Lamb does not like to hear her friends arguing. "I don't know," she says nervously.

Proud Peacock closes his feathers like a fan. "You are just jealous of my beauty," he tells his friends. "I am finished with all of you." And he tiptoes off into the forest.

Unfortunately, Proud Peacock is very angry and is not being careful. Suddenly, he finds he cannot walk anymore. "I think I am stuck," he says. He turns around. His tailfeathers are caught in a bramble bush! Proud Peacock tugs to get free.

"My beautiful feathers will get all torn," he cries as he pulls harder and harder.

But it is no use. Finally, he stops trying. He waits and waits. It is getting dark and he is very hungry. "Being handsome is certainly not getting me out of this," he thinks sadly.

Suddenly, he sees Gentle Lamb prancing toward him. "I am so glad to see you," says Proud Peacock.

"I was worried," says Gentle Lamb. "I came to see if you were all right." And then she sees Proud Peacock's tail. "Oh, dear," says Gentle Lamb, and she tries to pull the bramble bush away from Proud Peacock's tail. But she is not strong enough. "Wait," she says. "I will get Hungry Bear and Slow Turtle."

Soon Gentle Lamb and Hungry Bear come back. Hungry Bear is carrying Slow Turtle. "We couldn't wait for him to get here by himself," explains Hungry Bear, setting Slow Turtle down near the bramble bush. "What's the problem?"

"The problem is obvious," says Slow Turtle. "Now, I will get under the bush and tell you where to pull the brambles apart," he says to Hungry Bear. "The brambles won't hurt my leathery skin."

Slow Turtle crawls under the bush. "Lift the top bramble off the tail first," he directs Hungry Bear. "And then lower the bramble under the tail."

"Ouch," says Hungry Bear. "These brambles are sharp." But he follows Slow Turtle's directions. Then Gentle Lamb carefully lifts Proud Peacock's tail from between the two brambles —and Proud Peacock is free!

"Thank you," says Proud Peacock to his friends. "I never could have done it without you. Well, I guess being beautiful does not solve every problem."

Then, very slowly, he spreads his tailfeathers. "Are they all right?" he asks. "Are they as beautiful as they were before?"